MW00966643

Periwinkle Isn't Paris

MARILYN EISENSTEIN
Illustrated by Rudolf Stüssi

Tundra Books

Text copyright © 1999 by Marilyn Eisenstein
Illustrations copyright © 1999 by Rudolf Stüssi

Published in Canada by Tundra Books,
McClelland & Stewart Young Readers,
481 University Avenue, Toronto, Ontario M5G 2E9

Published in the United States by Tundra Books
of Northern New York,
P.O. Box 1030, Plattsburgh, New York 12901

Library of Congress Catalog Number: 99-70967

All rights reserved. The use of any part of this publication reproduced, transmitted in any form or by any means, electronic, mechanical, photocopying, recording, or otherwise, or stored in a retrieval system, without the prior written consent of the publisher – or, in case of photocopying or other reprographic copying, a licence from the Canadian Copyright Licensing Agency – is an infringement of the copyright law.

Canadian Cataloguing in Publication Data

Eisenstein, Marilyn
    Periwinkle isn't Paris

ISBN 0-88776-451-7

I. Stüssi, Rudolf. II. Title.

PS8559.I83P47 1999   jC813'.54   C99-930628-6
PZ7.E34675Pe 1999

We acknowledge the support of the Canada Council for the Arts and the Ontario Arts Council for our publishing program.

We acknowledge the financial support of the Government of Canada through the Book Publishing Industry Development Program for our publishing activities.

Canadä

Design by Sari Ginsberg

Printed and bound in Hong Kong, China

1 2 3 4 5 6   04 03 02 01 00 99

For my family
— M.E.

For my sons, Errol and Max, and in memory of
my mother, the Swiss illustrator Anita Dios-Bebié
— R.S.

The sidewalks of Periwinkle are lined with blue flowers shaped like tiny stars. But Polly doesn't notice.

Polly loves Paris. She loves French fries, French bread, French toast, French pastry, French dressing, French doors, French horns, French harps, and French poodles (and Polly's afraid of dogs).

"Can we go to Paris, please?" Polly pleads with her mother at least twice a day. And all Polly hears her mother say is, "Someday, Polly, someday. For now, Periwinkle will just have to do."

One sunny summer Sunday, when the
Periwinkle sky was a perfect French blue,
Polly announced: "You must call me Paulette.
It is the French version of my name."

Her brother, Benji, teased: "Paulette, Paulette,
Paulette, Paulette, can you make me an
omelette?" Polly could hear her mother's
laughter through the doorway.

"No one understands," Polly grumbled. She picked up her kitten, Pierrette, and clomped up the stairs to her room. She called Clementine, Her Very Best Friend and Next-Door Neighbor, to come over at once.

"Don't tell me. You want to go to Paris." Clementine had heard this one hundred times before.

"Paris, yes, it has to be Paris . . . only Paris," Polly sighed.

"What's so special about Paris?" Clementine had asked this question one hundred times before.

"Absolutely everything," Polly answered. "The Eiffel Tower shining against the blue Paris sky. The bookstalls along the Seine. The outdoor cafés, with café au lait and fresh croissants. . . ." Polly's eyes sparkled like periwinkles. "I wish I could be there now!"

"Let's run away." Polly closed her eyes and pretended that her bed was a boat, sailing the seas to France.

Clementine jumped thoughtfully from corner to corner on Polly's bedroom carpet. "Mmm. It's summer vacation. Perhaps we *could* leave Periwinkle. . . . First, we'll take a bus to the ocean. From there, we'll find a luxury ocean liner and secretly climb on board." She flopped down next to Polly.

"And voilà! We are in Paris," Polly whooped. She could almost hear the accordion players on the cobblestone streets. "Oh, Clem, let's leave tomorrow."

"It's not going to be easy, but okay," Clementine said.

They linked fingers and shook their secret handshake.

That night Polly stuffed her lucky blue chemise, a cream cotton cardigan, a blue silky scarf, cat's-eye sunglasses, a French blue beret, a Paris guidebook, all her saved allowance, and a family portrait into her faded green gym bag.

She piled all her postcards of Paris and her Paris books – ten of her own and five from the library – in the corner of her room. Carefully, she took the bright blue ribbons from her hair and arranged it into a chignon. "Far more Parisian," she said aloud, with a happy nod in the mirror.

Then, she pinned a note to the petit point pillow on her bed, removed the pins from her hair, and fell asleep:

Dearest Maman,
I hope that you won't be angry, but
Clementine and I are on our way to Paris.
I'm not running away because I'll be back.
       Je t'aime,
       Paulette
       xxxxxxx
P.S. Please feed my goldfish. Anouk
(the one with the yellow stripe) needs
more food than André.

As Polly lay sleeping, she dreamed of buses and ocean liners and Paris. She felt a warm wind play with her hair as she and Clementine waved good-bye. "Adieu, Periwinkle. . . ."

The next morning Polly and Clementine raced to the
bus. "Welcome aboard," announced the driver, wiping
his brow like a salute. Polly gave a happy bounce. The
door clanged shut, and they were on their way.

Periwinkle grew smaller through the window. Polly groped for the sandwich she'd made that morning and offered it to Clementine. "Pretend it's Brie on a baguette."

"No, thanks," she said with a sniff.

The girls rode in silence. But as the bus took them further and further away from Periwinkle, a strange thing happened. Polly stopped thinking about Paris.

Instead, she thought about Pierrette's damp nose nuzzling her cheek. She thought about her mother's flapjacks; how the sweet cinnamon smell reached all the way up to the attic. She thought about Benji sitting at the table, with Pierrette on his lap and flapjacks on his plate. She thought about the periwinkles, tiny blue stars, lining the sidewalks to her home.

The bus bounced to a halt. "This is as far as I go, girls. I'm heading back to Periwinkle. You're going to have to take another bus," the driver said, adjusting his cap.

Polly turned to Clementine. "I can't go to Paris. I'm not ready. I would miss everyone too much."

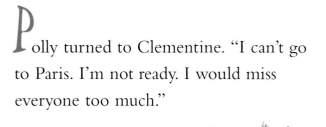

"What a relief! Don't worry. We'll go to Paris when we're older." They linked fingers and shook their secret handshake.

They all got out of the bus and stretched their legs. "Will you take us back to Periwinkle?" Clementine asked the driver. He nodded, as if he shared their secret.

"This is the end of the line, girls," the bus driver announced as he passed the town sign. Polly looked out the window and could see her special tree, the store where they knew her name, and billowy clothes on clotheslines waving like flags, welcoming them back to Periwinkle.

"Race you home," Clementine said to Polly.

"Adieu," Polly called to the bus driver.

"Au revoir," he shouted in reply.

Polly ran along the sidewalks of Periwinkle to her mother's waiting arms. "Welcome home, Paulette. I saved you some flapjacks." Her mother hugged her tight.